Dog!

Dog!

PRUDENCE ANDREW

Illustrated by TREVOR STUBLEY

THOMAS NELSON INC.
Nashville / Camden / New York

Text copyright © 1968, 1973 by Prudence Andrew
Illustrations copyright © 1968, 1973 by Trevor Stubley

First U.S. edition

All rights reserved under International and Pan-American Conventions. Published by Thomas Nelson Inc., Nashville, Tennessee. Manufactured in the United States of America.

Library of Congress Cataloging in Publication Data

Andrew, Prudence
    Dog!

    SUMMARY: A ten-year-old boy who is forbidden to have a dog finds a stray and hides him in an abandoned car.
    [1. Dogs—Stories]   I. Stubley, Trevor, illus.
II. Title.
PZ7.A5595Do3   [Fic]   72-12920
ISBN 0-8407-6272-0
ISBN 0-8407-6273-9 (lib. bdg.)

Dog!

1

"Come on, boy," said Andrew Thornton to his dog.

Andrew's friend John paused while Andrew waited for his dog to sniff around a lamppost. This was very nice of John, because Andrew's dog was imaginary. Andrew was ten years old and for as long as he could remember he had longed for a dog. But he'd never been able to have a real dog, only an imaginary one.

"Good dog," said Andrew.

The boys walked on, puffing out steam into the freezing air. Andrew's sister Anne and John's sister Jenny, who were younger than the boys, skipped ahead. It was a Saturday morning in February. They were going to the children's film show in the center of the town. They were in the middle of the housing project where they all lived, walking toward the bus stop.

It was an incredibly clean housing project. The roads were smooth and the sidewalks spotless. Velvet green grass stretched in front of the houses. Every twenty yards a neat little tree sprouted out of the curb. In the pale winter light the houses looked like toy houses, each with its brightly painted front door. There wasn't a cardboard box or a can or a bit of litter to be seen. The wives cleaning their windows wore starched aprons. The husbands washing their spotless cars wore home-made pullovers.

On the corner Andrew stopped to let his imaginary dog cock his leg. He looked at John, very neat in his blue windbreaker and his shiny shoes. He looked at Anne and Jenny, spruce and gay in their colored socks and pompom hats. He looked at the bus line, all in their go-to-town clothes. He looked down at himself, at his dusty shoes, his crumpled jeans, his duffle coat rubbed at the seams.

"I don't know how you get so messy," his mother kept telling him. "Why can't you stay neat like Anne? I wash and mend your things and they're torn again in two minutes. And comb your hair, it looks like a haystack."

Andrew sighed. He hated the housing project because it was so clean and because all the people were so proper and prim. But most of all he hated it because nobody in the project was allowed to keep a dog. It was a rule. No dogs in the housing project. The only dog Andrew Thornton was allowed to have was an imaginary dog.

"The bus is coming," said John.

Andrew jerked his dog's lead and they all ran

across the road. The bus line stirred. There was a young woman with a rigid hairdo, two little children in dazzling white socks, their mother in a fake fur coat, and a black-coated, black-hatted man carrying a rolled-up black umbrella.

The bus swung around the corner.

At this exact moment a little dog ran in front of the bus. The bus screeched to a stop. The dog disappeared under the bus, then shot out from behind the front wheels. He came racing toward the bus line.

"Here, boy," called Andrew, snapping his fingers. The little dog bounded straight toward him. "Here, boy."

Out into the road rushed the man with the umbrella. He raised his umbrella and whacked the dog on the back. The dog squealed, swerved, and fled away up the road.

Anger boiled up inside Andrew. He shouted at the umbrella man, "You shouldn't have hit him."

"Teach it a lesson," said the man, inspecting his umbrella for damage.

"You shouldn't hit dogs," Andrew protested. He turned in appeal to the people on the bus line.

"You can't go hitting dogs," said John loyally.

"Teach it a lesson," repeated the umbrella man.

"Can't have dogs running all over the place," said the young woman, patting her hair.

"Dogs aren't allowed around here anyway," said the mother.

"That's right," said the umbrella man. "There's a rule. No dogs."

"They're a menace," said the bus conductor.

"Ought to be a law," shouted the bus driver from his cab.

Andrew was nearly in tears. He could not forget the dog's squeal of pain and the way he had rushed away with his tail between his legs. Such a nice little dog, too. Brown and white, with pricked-up ears and short legs. "You shouldn't hit dogs," he declared.

Everyone got on the bus. Andrew went and sat down up front.

"Aren't you going to the back, Andrew?" John asked. Andrew always went to the back because of his imaginary dog.

But Andrew had forgotten about his imaginary dog. He sat staring at the steamy window and thought about the real dog he had just seen.

To comfort him, his friend John said, "I bet that dog's found his way home all right. I don't think he was really hurt." Andrew said nothing. John rubbed a clear place on the window. "Look, there's a Great Dane, Andrew. Look."

"It's a Labrador," said Andrew, but he didn't sound very interested.

John couldn't understand it. Normally Andrew goggled out of the window at every dog he saw.

Soon the bus reached the busy part of the town. It passed the street where Andrew used to live with his family, in an apartment on the top floor of an old house. He had lived there for nine years, until his dad had managed to get a house in the spick-and-span housing project. Andrew hadn't been able to keep a dog in the apartment either, because the landlady wouldn't let him. In all his ten years he had never been allowed to have a real dog.

"Here we are," said John.

The two boys and their sisters got off. Andrew looked gloomy. He was still worrying about the little dog. John noticed that Andrew was no longer holding his arm stiff. This meant that Andrew no longer had his imaginary dog with him. It was astonishing. Andrew took his imaginary dog everywhere, even to the movies.

They joined the line of children outside the movies. It was very cold. A sharp wind set them all shivering.

"There's a nice poodle," said John, who preferred cars.

Andrew didn't even turn his head.

When the doors opened, all the children rushed in. Andrew and John and the girls sat in their favorite seats in the front row upstairs. They seldom missed a Saturday morning movie show. John liked the serials, which were always about a group of children having impossible adventures. The girls liked the cartoons and the funny men. And Andrew? Andrew went for the dog films. There was always a dog film of some sort, about a fabulous German shepherd, or a sheep dog who saved his master from Indians, or a terrier who stole sausages.

This week the dog film was called *Dogs' Home*. It was about a refuge for stray dogs. The screen was filled with dogs of all shapes and kinds, spotted dogs, dappled dogs, pedigreed dogs, mongrel dogs like the dog under the bus. A boy looked after these stray dogs. He had a favorite, a rough little terrier like the dog under the bus.

Andrew said aloud, "I bet that man hurt him."

When the film ended he said, "When I have a dog I'm going to have a dog just like that."

For the hundredth time John said, "But you can't have a dog. Where we live, nobody can have a dog. You can only have birds and goldfish and tortoises."

"I'm going to have a dog," said Andrew. "I *am* going to have a dog. A real dog."

The serial film started. Andrew wasn't interested in the serial, because there wasn't a dog in it. He sat back in his seat and watched the silver beams of the projector shifting in the darkness above him. He thought about the little dog. Where had he come from? Where did he run to when the man hit him? Had he anywhere to sleep? Would *he* be taken to a dog's pound?

Then Andrew heard a dog barking. Hurriedly he sat up. There was a red setter on the screen, barking. It was a stupid story really. Two brothers of ten and eleven lived in Canada, on the edge of a forest. They longed for a baby sister, but they didn't have one. One day they found a baby girl abandoned in tall grass. They hid her in the forest, in a shelter they built for her. They kept her there for weeks. In this episode, some grownups found the shelter and the baby. The red setter belonged to one of the grown-ups.

As soon as the red setter went off the screen, Andrew lost interest and thought about the little dog again.

At noon the children came out into the street. It was colder than ever. An icy wind blew. They crossed the street and waited for a bus. Again Andrew sat in the front and stared at the steamy window. The bus started, stopped, jolted along the busy streets.

John said, "What's the matter?"

Andrew said, "I'm going to find that dog."

2

"I'm going to find that dog," said Andrew.
"But he ran away."
"I'll look for him."
"But he may be miles and miles away."
"I'm going to look for him," said Andrew stubbornly.
"What'll you do if you find him? You can't keep him. They won't let people have dogs where we live."
"I'll think of something."
"You'll have to take him to the police station."
"They'd put him to sleep."
"Dog shelter, then."
"They put dogs to sleep, too, if no one wants them."
"Someone would want him, I bet," said John.
But Andrew didn't want someone else to have the little brown-and-white terrier. He wanted to have him himself.
"I'll help you look," said John.
"Thanks," said Andrew.
They got off the bus. The sky was a curious

whitish color. Everybody they saw was breathing out a cloud of smoke. The two girls ran ahead. Andrew did not lead his imaginary dog.

"When are you going to start looking?" asked John.

"After lunch."

"See you then."

Andrew walked up his front path. His house had a bright-yellow front door. The doorstep was dazzling white. Every window was draped in frilly white curtains, because Andrew's mother was very proud of her house. Andrew went around to the back. He opened the door and stepped into the hallway. He changed into his slippers and hung up his duffle coat. He went into the kitchen. His mother was frying sausages. The bow of her apron was in the exact center of her waist.

Andrew started, "Mom, there was a dog—"

"Be quick, there's a good boy. Your dad wants to be off. And comb your hair. I don't know how you get so messy. Your hands are filthy."

"Mom, there was this dog—"

"Nasty dirty things, making messes all over the place. If there's one thing I can't stand, it's dog messes on the sidewalk."

This was one reason Andrew's mother had been so eager to move to the development, or so Andrew thought. It was because there were no dogs.

He gave up trying to tell her about the little dog. He washed his hands and combed his hair with his fingers. His father came into the kitchen and they sat down and ate their sausages and potatoes and dessert. Andrew dropped some food on his shirt and his mother fussed with a wet cloth, getting it off. Then she went into the hall to get out the vacuum cleaner.

Andrew's father rose and put on his cap. In desperation Andrew blurted out, "Can I have a dog? Please can I? Just a little one. He couldn't jump the fence at the back. Please."

"There's no use carrying on, son. If I let you have a dog, we'd be out on our ears in a month.

No dogs. That's the rule. I've told you a hundred times. We'd lose the house.''

"But Dad—"

"I'm off," said his father. He lit a cigarette, resettled his cap, and went off to his football game.

Andrew's mother bustled back to clear the dishes. "If you've nothing better to do than sulk, Andrew, you can give me a hand with the bedrooms. Your room is a real mess, I've never seen such a shambles. Why can't you keep your room neat like Anne? I've told you—"

Andrew retreated to the hallway. He put on his shoes and his duffle coat and his gloves and his warm hood. He checked to make sure that his string was in his pocket. He always carried string, in case he found a stray dog.

John was waiting outside, blue with cold. Together they walked to the corner. Andrew's arms swung free; he was not leading a dog.

"Where are you going to look?" asked John.

"There," said Andrew, pointing the way the little dog had run.

They turned left and walked past dozens of neat houses, glued together in pairs. No dog would have found a refuge here, among these shiny homes.

John said, "Where does this go to?"

Andrew didn't know.

They walked on, hunched against the icy wind.

Suddenly the smooth road ended, as if it had been cut off with a pair of scissors. Beyond, there was a mess of potholes, stones, sand, mud, gravel, bricks, planks, building machinery, and half-completed houses. Andrew stared into the distance. Beyond the building site he saw country. He saw a hedge, a gate, a green hill and, on the skyline, a brown wood. "I bet he went that way," he said.

He picked his way over the frozen mud. John followed. On the left was one completed pair of houses. The right-hand house had curtains at the windows. "We could ask," said John.

Andrew pressed the doorbell, which went *ding-dong*. The front door opened and a large man demanded, "What d'you want?" He wore a vest with silver buttons. The backs of both his hands were tattooed with blue faces. "What d'you want?" he growled.

A woman's voice screeched, "Shut that door!"

"Have you seen my dog?" Andrew asked. "He's brown and white and—"

"No, I have not," snapped the man; and he slammed the door in Andrew's face.

They went on, over ice-filled potholes and frozen mounds of mud, toward the gate and the green field. From the depths of his hood John said, "We could ask somewhere else."

"Nowhere to ask," said Andrew.

But there was.

3

At the end of the building site, next to the hedge, stood another completed pair of houses. The nearer house was empty, but the farther one was occupied, because smoke swirled out of the chimney. Andrew hesitated. He dreaded facing another big, angry man. Then he thought of the little dog out in the cold, and he took courage. He picked his way to the front door. Then he changed his mind and went around to the back. John followed. There was no bell, no knocker. Andrew banged with his gloved fist. Nothing happened. He banged again. The handle turned. The door scraped open. In the doorway stood a young woman with a baby in her arms.

She asked, "What's the matter, son?"

Andrew sighed with relief. She was smiling! She had blue curlers in her hair and red bedroom slippers on her feet. Her baby's face was covered with chocolate.

Andrew said, "I've lost my dog. Have you seen him?"

"What's he like?"

"He's small and he's white with brown patches. Rough-coated. With short legs."

"I've seen him!" she exclaimed.

"Where? Where?"

"I've seen him once or twice. In the field."

Andrew was stammering with excitement. "D-did you see him this m-morning?"

"You'd better come in," said the young woman, opening the door wider. "You look frozen, the pair of you."

"No, thanks," said Andrew, who was dying to be off. "We've got to look for him."

The young woman called after them, "Let me know if you find him. I'll be on the lookout."

"Thanks," shouted Andrew into the wind.

They climbed over the gate. They found the field was enclosed by a thick hedge. "Up there," said Andrew, pointing up the slope toward the wood.

They plodded up the slope, slipping on the frosty grass. They found a thin place in the hedge. Andrew forced a way through, tearing his jeans. John followed, tearing nothing. Andrew led the way into the wood. It was ghostly. They sank ankle deep in dead leaves. Over their heads, branches scraped and creaked. A big gray bird clapped away into the sky. Andrew's teeth chattered. His feet felt like blocks of wood. His fingertips ached. He never doubted, not for an instant, that the little dog was somewhere near. He never doubted that Andrew Thornton would find him and save him from starvation and exposure.

"He can't be here," whispered John.

"He could sleep in holes."

"What holes?"

"Fox holes."

"What would he eat?"

"Rabbits."

"Bet you he's not here."

"Bet you he is."

Andrew called, "Here, boy. Where are you, boy?" He searched the whole wood, calling and whistling. But no little dog appeared. Above the trees, the sky changed from white to gray. Still Andrew searched and called.

From a distance John shouted, "Andrew! Come and look."

Andrew hurried to him. John was on the far edge of the wood, staring down at a stream. The stream looked black and fast. Beyond it stretched a big field.

"Look at that," said John, pointing.

"That" was an old wheelless car, abandoned on the far side of the stream.

"Let's have a look," said John, who was crazy about cars.

"He couldn't get across the water," said Andrew.

But when they got down to the stream they found a few stones sticking up out of the water. A brave and agile little dog could cross on flat-topped stones like these. Andrew and John crossed on the stones. John got one of the car doors open. All the seats were gone, but the windows were intact. John crouched inside, making engine noises and twiddling the steering wheel. Andrew explored the big field and lane beyond. He roamed around until it was nearly dark. He called until his throat was sore. But no dog came.

At last Andrew gave up. But only for that day. He said, "I'm going to look again. I'm going to search every day until I find Pooper."

"Who?"

"Pooper."

"Is that the dog?"

"Yes. Pooper. That's what I'm going to call him."

Andrew arrived home frozen and purple. His mother sent him up to have a hot bath. By the time he came down she had discovered the tear in his jeans. She nagged poor Andrew about this until even Andrew's father got fed up and said, "Stop already, Joan. Boys are boys, when all's done. If I had a ten for every time I tore my pants, I'd be a rich man." He blew two smoke rings, one through the other.

Andrew escaped early to bed. He could not sleep. He heard the wind whistling and he saw a picture of Pooper cowering in some hole in the wood. "I'll find you, Pooper," he swore. "I'll search and search until I find you."

Andrew searched. He searched all day Sunday. He searched every afternoon after school until it became too dark to see. Every day he called at the Walterses' house. (The young woman with the baby was Mrs. Walters.) He saw Mr. Walters, too, who was the image of the baby. But neither of them had seen Pooper again. Every evening Andrew returned home miserable and frozen with cold. Naturally his mother wanted to know where he and John were going off to all the time.

"Just playing," said Andrew. "We've found an old car."

"But you get so cold," complained his mother. "And you've got those horrid chilblains."

"Nothing wrong in playing in an old car," said Andrew's father. "Played in dozens when I was a boy."

"But he'll catch pneumonia."

"Not if he takes hot baths."

"But he makes the bathtub so dirty. He never scrubs it out."

"Stop it, Joan. A house is for living in, after all. Let the boy play in his precious car."

So Andrew was able to go on searching the fields and the wood for Pooper. He never asked himself what he would do when he found him. He *would* find him. That was enough.

Tuesday. Wednesday. Thursday. Friday. Saturday. Sunday. Every day Andrew and John went up the slope and through the hedge and through the wood and across the stream. Andrew called and searched and whistled, and John played in the car. But they found no dog. By Sunday evening even Andrew was losing faith. Perhaps Pooper had gone for good. Perhaps the umbrella man had scared him off. Perhaps he was miles away, or snug in his own home.

Next morning was Monday. Andrew overslept. His mother came in to wake him. She walked over to the window. She said, "Who'd have thought it? There wasn't anything about it on the news." She came to the bed and prodded Andrew's feet. Andrew opened his eyes. His ceiling was shining with a strange light. He got out of bed and went to the window.

The world was smothered in snow.

4

Pooper!

It was the first thing Andrew thought of—Pooper out in the snow. He couldn't enjoy the shining snow. He couldn't enjoy the sky, which had turned blue overnight, as if someone had painted it. He couldn't enjoy the sun, which was glowing like a big yellow bulb in the sky. As he trudged to school in three pairs of socks and his boots, he hadn't the heart to throw snowballs or take a ride on Peter Johnson's sled. He hadn't the heart to join in John's plans to build a snowman or to run after the bulldozer as it piled the snow into the gutters with its shovel. He could think of nothing but Pooper lost in the snow.

"Well, you can't do anything now," said John.

"Oh, can't I?" thought Andrew; but he said nothing.

As soon as school was over, Andrew hurried away without waiting for John. He went past rows of houses where housewives in fur boots and head scarves were shoveling away the snow and sprinkling ashes and salt. He went past the bus stop where he had seen Pooper beaten by the umbrella man. He reached the end of the cleared road. Now he had to struggle over snowy humps and through snowy pits and past snow-draped timber and tractors.

The sun shone. The snow sparkled. The sky was as blue as bluebells. The cold was brisk and joyful. Andrew should have been enjoying himself. But he could think only of Pooper, of Pooper falling asleep exhausted in the snow and dying there, like a traveler in an adventure book. He plunged on, not caring when the snow filled his boots and melted there. He was too distressed to call at the Walterses'. He floundered over mounds and through troughs until at last he reached the gate. He climbed over it, knocking a powder of snow off the gate bars. He trudged up the hill, heaving his sodden boots one after another. Up and up he plodded, panting and sweating. His legs ached and his toes squelched inside his three pairs of soaked socks. He reached the hedge and climbed wearily through it, tearing a hole in his school pants. He plunged into the wood. He fell waist-deep into a hollow. He hauled himself out by a tree root. He felt the snow sneaking in through the gap between his pants and his shirt. He called, "Pooper! Poo-per! Where are you, boy? Come on, it's only me."

The miracle happened.

A little dog came out from behind a tree. He began struggling toward Andrew through the snow, his head held high as if he were swimming. Andrew stood, frozen in the act of stuffing his shirt into his pants. He couldn't call. He couldn't move. He couldn't whistle. He watched the little dog fight his way through the snowdrifts toward him. The dog was six yards away, four yards, two yards—all Andrew could see of him was a pair of ears sticking up like two tiny triangular brown flags and two dark eyes and a black nose with a crusting of snow. The little dog was only a yard away. Andrew lunged forward with his arms outstretched. With a final effort the little dog reached him. Andrew's arms closed around him and together they rolled over and over in the snow, Andrew clutching the dog and the dog whining and licking his cheek.

"Pooper!" cried Andrew. "Oh, Pooper!" And he burst into tears because he was so happy and so relieved.

He sat up and held Pooper and looked at him. Pooper was just as he remembered him, dirty white patched with brown. He had a frill of hair sticking out around his neck, and he had short legs and a stiff little tail. Pooper's tail was not between his legs now; it was wagging so fast it looked like half a dozen tails. In delight, Andrew examined Pooper's tufty brown eyebrows and his bright-pink tongue and his eyes, which were black, with a star in each one. But how thin he was! Under the shaggy coat Andrew could feel Pooper's ribs, like railings.

Pooper sneezed, blowing the snow off his nose.

Andrew brought out of his pocket the sugar lumps he had been saving. He offered one to Pooper. Pooper snatched it between his teeth and crunched ravenously. His syrupy spit dribbled onto Andrew's hand. When Pooper had gobbled up all the sugar lumps, Andrew unbuttoned his coat and fastened Pooper snugly inside. Pooper needed no pulling; he wriggled into Andrew's coat as if there were nowhere in the world he would rather be. Andrew got up. He felt Pooper's nose wet and cold on his neck. He leaned against a tree. Pooper began to shiver. He shivered so violently that Andrew's whole body shook and a lump of snow fell with a plop off a branch of the tree.

"Never mind, Pooper. I'll soon get you nice and warm. And I'll give you a lovely meal. I bet you're hungry. Where've you been all this time? Never mind. I'll look after you. I won't let that horrible umbrella man hurt you."

What could he do? Oh, what could he do? Where could he take Pooper? He couldn't take him home. His mother would have a fit and his father would explain for the umpteenth time that they would lose their house if they kept a dog. His father would make him take Pooper down to the police station. Pooper would be shut up in a beastly kennel. He'd be put to sleep if no one claimed him. Andrew felt Pooper's neck. No collar, no address. He couldn't help feeling pleased. As long as Pooper had no address, he belonged to nobody. As long as he belonged to nobody, he belonged to Andrew Thornton. But where was Andrew Thornton to take him?

Andrew hitched Pooper's front paws onto his shoulder. He waded to the edge of the wood and climbed through the hedge. The snow was melting inside his clothes, but he did not feel it. He had no ideas. All he knew was that he had found Pooper and he was not going to let him go. He would find some place to keep him even if he had to run away to do it. He buried his face in Pooper's ruff. He lifted his head. The sun was gone. Oddly, the world looked suddenly brown. He gazed down at the half-built houses beyond the gate. Smoke rose in a poker-straight line from the Walterses' chimney. The Walterses! Of course. They would help him. They would help Pooper.

Andrew ran down the hill, throwing up his legs to get them clear of the snow. He fell. He struggled up with Pooper still secure inside his coat. He climbed the gate. He made his way to the Walterses' back door, stepping in Mr. Walterses' outgoing footprints.

He knocked.

5

The door was opened by Mrs. Walters and the dimpled baby. She looked at Andrew, then at his precious burden. She smiled and exclaimed, "Oh, you've found him. I'm so glad. Won't you be glad to get home, boy. Eh, boy?" And she rubbed Pooper behind the ears.

Andrew began, "He was in—" Then he stopped, because he realized something. Mrs. Walters thought Pooper was *his* dog. Really his dog. She thought Pooper had strayed from Andrew's home. She thought that Andrew was now going to take Pooper home to a big fire and a tasty meal and a rejoicing family.

He said, "Pooper doesn't come from my house."

She said, "What do you mean? I thought he was your dog. I thought you'd lost him."

Andrew said, "Well, you see . . ."

She said, "Come on in. No sense in standing on the doorstep."

Andrew carried Pooper into the kitchen. Mrs. Walters strapped the baby into his highchair. She gave him a cookie, but he was far more interested in the messy little creature that emerged from Andrew's coat and stood, shivering, on the kitchen table among the jars and the bottles. Andrew put his hand on Pooper's wet back and the whole of his arm became warm and the warmth spread all over him.

Pooper made a dive for a loaf of bread. Andrew caught him. "Have you got any milk?" he asked. Mrs. Walters edged sideways between an iron and a clothes basket. She opened the top of a cupboard and out fell a package of cornflakes, spilling all over the floor. Pooper jumped off the table and began frantically licking up cornflakes. Mrs. Walters brought a bottle of milk to the table, and a bowl from the sink. Andrew tore a slice of bread to pieces and put it in the bowl. He poured milk on top of it and set the bowl on the floor. Pooper rushed to the bowl and began gulping and lapping, making little noises of delight. He stood straddled on his four short legs, his tail stuck up at a right angle, guzzling bread and milk. From time to time he lifted his head and looked around as if to say, "I'm only stopping for a breather." Then he ran his tongue over his chops to collect all the stray drops of milk, and buried his nose in the bowl again.

Andrew crouched beside him on the floor, crumbling bread and pouring milk. Soon, Pooper's belly felt like a blown-up balloon. All of a sudden he flopped down and let his head fall on Andrew's knee. Andrew stroked Pooper's rough head. He could hear milk gurgling inside Pooper's stomach.

"I thought he was yours," said Mrs. Walters with her hand on the kettle.

"Well, you see . . ." And Andrew launched into his story of the bus and the umbrella man and the stream and the old car.

"Are you going to take him home?" asked Mrs. Walters as she poured boiling water into the teapot.

Andrew took a deep breath. He said, "Could you keep him for me? Just for tonight. While I think of something." Mrs. Walters stood looking

down at him with the big brown teapot in her
hand. Andrew pleaded, "I can't take him home.
My mother would have a fit. You see, we live in
the project, right in the middle. But you could
keep him, couldn't you? Just for one night. No
one would know, not out here."

Mrs. Walters put the teapot on the table. She
sat down. She said, "But this is the development
too, son. No one here can keep a dog. I'd love
to have your dog, really." *Your dog*. It sounded
so lovely that Andrew felt warm all over.

Mrs. Walters leaned down and smoothed Pooper's head. She said, "I love dogs. We always had
a dog at home."

"Bet you didn't live in a project then," said
Andrew.

"Well, it was a project. But an old one, not a
bit like this. People could have dogs there because
the houses were so old and the place was so shabby.
My mother had a dog right up till I got married.
Ruffie his name was. He was brown." She
handed Andrew a plate of cookies. Pooper licked
his lips in his sleep. Mrs. Walters poured two cups
of tea.

Andrew said, "Did your mother get rid of her
dog?" He simply could not believe that anybody
could be allowed to keep a dog and yet *not* keep
one.

"Well, she gets ill, you see. And Arnie—that's

my brother—he's nuts about his motorcycle, and
my father works for the railroad and he works
very long hours, so really my mother can't man-
age a dog."

"Did he die?" asked Andrew, laying his hand
on Pooper's warm, tight stomach.

"Who?"

"Ruffie. Your mother's dog."

"No. My aunt took him. She lives in the
country."

Andrew ate his cookie. He sipped his sweet tea.
He thought, "If I was allowed a dog, I'd never let
him go, never. I'd die before I'd send him away."
He looked at Mrs. Walters, who was wiping the
baby's face with a cloth. She was so young and
so nice. He said, "Please have Pooper. Please.
Just for one night."

"But I'm afraid of Mr. Elliot finding out. He'd
tell the management. He's not a very nice man,
that Mr. Elliot. I'm afraid we'd lose our house."

Andrew didn't need telling who Mr. Elliot was.
Mr. Elliot was the horrible man with tattooed
hands.

Mrs. Walters said, "You'd better take him to
the police station. I mean, he might belong to
somebody."

But Andrew didn't think so. Of course, he
didn't want to think so. "Please," he begged. "Just
for one night. I'll think of something, honest. I'll

come tomorrow right after school and I'll think of something."

"Okay," said Mrs. Walters with a sudden smile. "My husband will find him a box and he can sleep in here. Just for one night, remember."

"Oh, thank you!" cried Andrew.

He kissed Pooper and hurried home. By great good luck his mother had taken Anne to have her hair cut, so Andrew was able to get all his wet clothes draped over the hot radiator without a scolding. He stuffed his wet boots with newspaper and wiped the hallway floor. He brushed and combed his hair and put on his jeans and a shirt and set the table. And all the time he was trembling with excitement and happiness.

His mother was amazed that he had set the table. "You *are* a good boy," she said. Luckily she didn't inspect Andrew's clothes on the radiator, so Andrew escaped to bed with nothing worse than, "Give your nails a good scrubbing and don't forget your chilblain ointment."

Andrew lay snug in bed and reveled in his joy that Pooper had been found. It was a beautiful calm night. A full moon stared in at the window. He wanted to do nothing but lie and watch it and think of his dog. *His dog.* But he knew he couldn't afford to waste time. He couldn't expect the Walterses to keep Pooper for long, not with Tattooed Elliot on the warpath. He must think of a plan.

He rolled on his back. In the moonlight the window frames threw rectangular patterns on the ceiling. What could he do? Where could he keep Pooper? The silver rectangles on the ceiling reminded him of something. What was it? Ah yes, the movie screen. All of a sudden Andrew remembered the film. Not the film about the dogs' home but the serial about the boys who kept a

baby in a shelter in the forest. If a boy could keep a baby for weeks without anyone knowing, surely a boy could keep a dog for months . . . forever. A dog was much less helpless than a baby.

Andrew sat up. Yes, that was it. He would keep Pooper in a secret place. Where? Suddenly he knew where. In the old car, of course. It was the perfect place. The car was dry and warm and out of the way. Its windows were intact, its doors fitted. Pooper would love it. Andrew could give him straw and he could sneak food to him and play with him after school, and then there would be the weekends and vacations. The Walterses would never tell. John would never tell. No one else would know.

Andrew lay back and gazed blissfully at the ceiling. He gave a deep sigh. He smiled. He turned on his side and fell into beautiful dreams.

6

Andrew got up very early and ironed his school pants. He stuck tape behind the tear in the seat so that it did not show. He made his bed and straightened up his room and cleaned the egg stain off his school shirt. When he went into the kitchen his mother said, "Well, I must say you look neat for once," and she fried Andrew two eggs.

John was waiting on the sidewalk, which Andrew's father had scraped clean of snow. The sun was shining. The air was marvelous. There wasn't a puff of wind. John said, "Where did you disappear to yesterday?"

Andrew swore John to secrecy. Then he explained about finding Pooper and leaving him for the night with Mrs. Walters. John was astonished and thrilled.

"You've got to help me," said Andrew.

"Course I will," said John. "It'll be super. Better than a film."

"Yes, it's going to be super," said Andrew, his eyes shining.

All day at school Andrew's head buzzed with

plans. He must buy dog food. A dog Pooper's
size would need a third of a big can of dog's meat
a day, besides bread or crackers. The bread he
could scrounge. Dog food cost twenty cents a
can. Andrew did sums on the cover of his English
book. Seven divided by three was two and a third
cans of dog food a week. Two and a third times
twenty cents was—well, it was about fifty cents a
week. Oh, dear. Andrew was given only twenty-
five cents a week allowance. Then he remembered his piggy bank. It held at least four dollars.
He could slide the coins out on a knife. How
many twenty cents were there in four dollars?
Andrew wrestled with this arithmetic. All the
time he was thinking, "What's he doing now?" or
"Has Mrs. Walters given him his lunch?" or
"What will Mrs. Walters do about letting him
out?"

Immediately after school Andrew and John hurried off to the Walterses'. Andrew was so excited
he fell into a hole and got his boots full of snow.
At the back door he pointed to two yellow stains
in the snow and said, "She let him out, then. I
hope Mr. Elliot didn't spot him."

Mrs. Walters invited them in. She didn't say,
"Take your boots off." She flung open the door
into the kitchen and cried, "Pooper! Here's your
master, Pooper." And Pooper came rushing out
from under the table and hurled himself into An-

drew's arms as if Andrew were the person he loved best in the whole world. Andrew hugged and kissed him and showed him proudly to John. He said, "Isn't he lovely? Isn't he marvelous?" His face shone.

Of course John hugged and admired Pooper, too. Mrs. Walters made cocoa, and they all sat around the table with their elbows among the dirty cups and the baby's half-sucked teething crackers. Andrew told her of his plan to keep Pooper in the old car. She was very excited, and bounced up and down until two of her curlers fell out. She said, "I could always give him a run mid-

day, seeing as you don't get home for lunch."
But somehow Andrew didn't feel very enthusiastic.
He wanted to do everything for Pooper himself.

He said, "Best not. He'll be okay, honest.
You've got the baby and all."

"Well, how can I help then?"

Andrew said, "Will you buy me some cans of
dog meat? It's twenty cents a can. I'll give you the
money tomorow."

Mrs. Walters promised she would. She also
promised Andrew lots of crusts and crackers and
anything else he might need. She said, "There's
straw around those piles of bricks, if you dig the
snow away." Really, she couldn't have been nicer.
She was the nicest grown-up Andrew had ever
met.

Andrew and John went out and scraped snow
away from the bricks and collected armfuls of
straw. They shook the snow off and piled the
straw onto Mrs. Walters' back porch. It was
taken for granted that Pooper was to stay one
more night with Mrs. Walters, while the straw
dried.

Pooper liked Mrs. Walters; Andrew could tell
by the way the dog looked at her with his head on
one side. But Andrew Thornton was his lord and
master. His bright black eyes kept coming back
to Andrew. He sat on Andrew's knees and kept
nudging Andrew's wrist with his nose. Even

when John offered him tidbits, he didn't jump off Andrew's lap. It was as if Pooper were the very dog Andrew had been waiting for all his life. It was as if Andrew were the very master Pooper had been waiting for all *his* life. Yet they were friends, too, as Andrew and John were friends.

At last Andrew tore himself away. He said, "You won't let that Mr. Elliot see him, will you? I'll bring the money tomorrow. And thanks ever so much."

"That's all right, son. I wish you could keep him at home, I do really."

"They'll never let people do what they want." Andrew sighed.

Outside, they heard voices and shouts. Appalled, they looked at one another. There were children in the field! They hurried to the gate and looked over. They saw a dozen children with toboggans and trays. Peter Johnson shouted, "Hi-ya, you two. Come and have a go on my sled."

In a panic Andrew said to John, "They'll find out!"

"They won't. They won't try and get through that hedge." John climbed the gate and went to have a ride on the sled.

"Don't tell!" whispered Andrew.

"What do you think I am?" said John.

Andrew pulled himself together. He realized that the tobogganing was a good thing. It made a good excuse for him to go to the field every day. Now that the sun was shining, even his mother could not object to him tobogganing with his friends. He could slip through the hedge when no one was looking and go through the wood and across the stream to Pooper. If he was missed, John would cover up for him. Good old John!

On their way home Andrew and John passed Mr. Walters, busy digging a way through the snow for his wife to wheel the carriage when she went out to buy Pooper's dog food. He gave Andrew a big wink. Andrew winked back. It was nice to be telling grown-ups what to do, for a change.

Andrew kicked off his boots in the hallway and went straight up to his bedroom. With a kitchen knife he wangled two nickels, a quarter, and five pennies out of the slit in his piggy bank.

"I can go tobogganing, can't I, Dad?" Andrew asked casually at supper.

"Of course you can, son. What are you going to toboggan on? Give him a tray, Joan. No money for toboggans when I was a boy." Andrew's father tipped back his chair and stared into his cigarette smoke, picturing himself as a boy on a tin tray.

Andrew's mother said, "Well, make sure you

get all your wet things off afterward, and change out of your school things before you go, and have a good hot bath and scrub the bathtub out. And don't take Anne tobogganing; she'll only get herself hit, those boys are so rough."

For the thousandth time Andrew felt that his mother wished he were a girl, a nice, tidy, helpful girl, instead of a lumping, scruffy boy. But this time he didn't let it worry him. His father had said he could go tobogganing, and he hadn't said *when*.

Next morning Andrew got up very early, before the sun had risen. He dressed silently in jeans and old sweaters, tied his money in a handkerchief, and stuffed it in a pocket. He tiptoed downstairs and he pulled on yesterday's damp boots. He took his mother's oldest tray, the big tin one with red roses on it, turned the key in the back door, and went out.

The sky was getting lighter, the snow whiter. He went quickly along the sidewalk, puffing out steam like an engine. He remembered leading an imaginary dog along this sidewalk. Now he did not need to, because he possessed a dog of his own. Pooper. Pooper. The name alone was enough to warm him.

At the corner he turned left, stepping over a pile of dirty snow. He reached the path Mr.

Walters had cleared for the carriage. He heard a sharp tearing sound. It was unmistakable. It was someone drawing a curtain. He looked up to the left. The sound came from Tattooed Elliot's house. Mr. Tattooed Elliott, in a white vest, was looking down at him!

7

Andrew hurried on. It was all he could do. He went straight past the Walterses' house without looking at it. He climbed the gate and hid behind the hedge until his heart had stopped thumping. Then he ran to the Walterses' back door and a few seconds later was safe inside their kitchen with Pooper in his arms.

Andrew had never felt so excited in his life. He barely tasted the cup of cocoa Mrs. Walters gave him. He untied his handkerchief and gave Mrs. Walters his forty cents. Mrs. Walters gave him a clock, two red plastic bowls, a can opener, and the baby's little sand spade. Andrew stuffed all these things down the front of his sweaters. Mrs. Walters gave Pooper a last bowl of bread and milk and a kiss. Mr. Walters went out in his pajamas to make sure the coast was clear and no Mr. Elliot was lurking nearby.

Andrew picked up the bundle of straw, which Mr. Walters had tied around with string. It was fairly dry. Andrew said to Mrs. Walters, "Thanks ever so much for helping me and Pooper."

"Go along with you," said Mrs. Walters, smiling. "I'll have the dog food for you when you get back."

"All clear," called Mr. Walters.

"Come on, boy," said Andrew.

Pooper couldn't believe his luck. He sat down and put his head on one side and looked at Andrew, at Mrs. Walters in her pink robe, at the open door, at Andrew loaded with straw.

"Come on, Pooper. Walk, boy. Come on, boy. Come and see your new house."

Pooper hesitated. Then he rushed out of the door and into the open, yelping with excitement. In an agony Andrew cried, "Ssh! Pooper, ssh!" The marvelous dog stopped yelping. It was obvious that he understood every word that Andrew said to him. He stopped barking but he still tore around and around, tossing up snow with his nose and digging with his hindlegs and rolling over and over in delight.

"Don't forget your tray," said Mrs. Walters, and she tucked it under Andrew's arm. "Goodbye, now."

"Bye," said Andrew.

He went out. "Come on, Pooper," he called. Pooper stopped rolling and digging and came to his master.

"Bye," said Mr. Walters.

"Bye," said Andrew.

"Bye," said the baby.

Together Andrew and Pooper went up the hill. It was crisscrossed with toboggan tracks and pitted by children's boots, so there was no fear of anyone noticing Pooper's pawmarks. At the top of the slope Andrew turned and looked down. He spotted Mr. and Mrs. Walters and the baby waving at their back door in their night things. He put down the straw and the tray and waved back.

Andrew climbed through the hedge and Pooper wriggled after him. They plodded through the wood—or rather, Andrew plodded and Pooper frisked like a lamb among daisies. They emerged, and Andrew looked down on the black stream and the expanses of white snow and the white mound that was the car.

"Well, here we are, Pooper," he said.

Pooper gave two sharp yaps. He knew it was safe to speak now.

They crossed the stream. While Pooper played in the snow, Andrew took out the baby's spade and dug away the snow from the nearside door. He left the rest untouched; it would help to keep the car warm. Pooper would be as snug as an Eskimo in an igloo.

Inside the car Andrew piled the straw into one corner. He filled one red plastic bowl from the stream and placed it where the front passenger's

feet would have been. The second red plastic bowl
he placed beside the gas pedal. He put the can
opener in the glove compartment. He wedged
the clock between the gas pedal and the foot
brake.

"Come on, Pooper," he called. "It's all ready."

Pooper poked his head in the door. He
sneezed, shook the snow off himself, then hopped
in. He ran round the inside of the car, sniffing in
all the corners. He jumped on the straw and

tossed it around with his nose. He ran to his bowl and took three laps. He went to Andrew, who was crouching under the steering wheel, and he put his paws on Andrew's chest and licked his cheek. Andrew breathed a sigh of relief. Pooper liked it.

What games they had! Andrew threw sticks for Pooper, and Pooper found them, however deep they had buried themselves. Andrew built a little snowman and Pooper knocked it to pieces. Andrew constructed a snow tunnel and Pooper crawled through it. When they were tired of the tunnel, they simply ran around and around in circles, shouting and barking, Pooper bouncing like a rubber ball in showers of snow.

At last Mrs. Walters' clock said eight o'clock. Andrew opened the car door and explained to Pooper that he must get in. "I'll be over later, Pooper. Don't worry, you'll be okay." Pooper drooped his head and looked up at Andrew from under his tufty eyebrows. He whined and backed away. "Come on, boy. It's nice and warm, honest. The time'll go very quickly."

Pooper whined again. Then he shook himself free of snow and jumped into the car. He trusted Andrew completely. Andrew looked at Pooper's paws to make sure there was no ice packed between the pads. He gave Pooper a kiss and a hug, said, "See you soon," and shut the door.

He walked quickly away with his tin tray. He
crossed the stream and trudged up to the wood,
stepping in his own tracks. He heard a yelp but
he went on. On the edge of the wood he looked
back. The car looked like an igloo with a black
front door. Something white bobbed at the window. It was Pooper, jumping to get a glimpse of
his master. Andrew felt suddenly afraid. When
those boys in the film kept the baby in the forest,

it had been summertime. Would Pooper be warm enough? Would his drinking water ice over? What if more snow fell and buried the car completely?

Andrew hurried through the wood. He slid three times down the slope on his mother's tin tray, in case Tattooed Elliot was on the lookout. The sun shone warm. The sky was blue. The snow sparkled whiter than white.

He ran home. His mother was in the kitchen. She had found the tear in his school pants. She was very cross. She said, "Why didn't you tell me? Oh yes, you did know. You've stuck tape over it, so you did know. I've been half an hour mending it and the cereal's not made yet and Anne's hair's not combed. Where on earth have you been? It's quarter past eight, and you know . . ."

Andrew said nothing. He always said nothing when his mother was in full flood. He held out his hand for his pants and his mother stopped talking to bite off a thread with her back teeth. As she gave him the pants, she said, "Well, you look pleased with yourself, I must say."

"Yes, tobogganing's super," said Andrew, and he rushed upstairs and changed so fast he had time to make his bed and straighten up his room and comb his hair. Now that he had this wonderful secret, it was very important to please his mother.

All day at school Andrew was so happy he

thought the top of his head would blow off. He wanted to shout aloud, "I've got a dog, I've got a dog!" He rushed home after school and changed into jeans and old sweaters, to save his school clothes. He collected John and, with his tin tray, hurried to the field. John went ahead and Andrew called at the Walterses for a can of dog meat.

"Everything all right?" asked Mrs. Walters, giving him the dog food and a bag of scraps.

"Fine," said Andrew, beaming. "Thanks ever so much."

He stuffed the bag of scraps into one pocket. He put the can of dog meat into the other. Taking his tray, he climbed up the slope through the crowd of playing and tobogganing children. He hung around near the hedge, awaiting his moment. John was getting all the big boys together for a race. Good for John! As soon as the trays and toboggans were halfway down the hill, Andrew scrambled through the hedge. He crouched on the far side. He peeped. No one seemed to have missed him.

He bounded through the wood. He burst out the other side and saw the car. He whistled, and a white shape bounced up behind the window. He hurled himself down the slope. He jumped from stone to stone across the stream. He wrenched open the door and Pooper shot like a cannonball into his arms.

They had a marvelous time. Pooper wolfed down his food. Andrew changed the drinking water and cleaned out the car. They played games in the snow until Andrew was exhausted. But not Pooper—Pooper was never exhausted. Andrew taught Pooper to beg. He taught him to balance a sugar lump on his nose; Pooper was an amazingly quick learner. When the sun disappeared and the air became gloomy, Andrew sat

in the car with Pooper on his lap and stroked his head and scratched the back of his ears.

All too soon the clock said a quarter to six. Andrew gave Pooper a last snack of crackers. He washed out the food bowl and rearranged the straw. He wound the clock. He kissed and hugged Pooper and said, "See you tomorrow morning, Pooper." He went away, shutting the car door. He did not look back.

As he made his way home he pictured all the dogs he had once been so crazy about, the German shepherds and sheepdogs in the Saturday-morning films, the town mongrels, the corgi who had lived near their apartment. He thought of the imaginary dog he used to take everywhere with him. Never again. He had Pooper. And Pooper was the cleverest, sweetest, bravest dog in the whole world.

8

Now began the most wonderful time of Andrew Thornton's life. Every morning he got up at dawn and dressed in his old clothes and took his tin tray and went to the field "to toboggan." And his mother could not stop him because his father said he could go.

On these mornings Andrew didn't wake the Walterses. He went straight through the wood and whistled and saw Pooper jump up at the car window. He rushed down and crossed over the stream and flung open the door and gathered Pooper in his arms. He fed Pooper crackers and bread crumbs and he cleaned out the car and changed the water and played lovely games with Pooper. No one came near them. There were no sounds from the distant cottages, no footprints in the lane. At eight o'clock Andrew said good-bye to Pooper and shut him up in the car. On the way home he tobogganed twice, for appearances' sake. Then he hurried home in time to straighten up his room and hang up his clothes and wash his face and brush his teeth and comb his hair and clean his shoes. Twice he even set the breakfast table. He tore no more holes in his pants. He kept the snow out of his boots. He no longer quarreled with Anne. He went to bed early. He scrubbed the bathtub. He cleaned his fingernails. He hummed and he sang.

"What's got into the boy?" his mother asked. "He's so neat and helpful, I can't believe it."

"The boy's growing up," Andrew's father replied. "I told you. Don't fence him in, I said, and you'll see how he'll blossom." Once, Andrew heard his father say to his mother, "Joan, have you noticed? Andrew doesn't carry on about having a dog anymore."

Andrew was certainly blossoming. His chilblains healed. His face turned rosy, then brown. He was always smiling, always happy. What a marvelous month it was! The sun shone like a Norwegian sun. The skies were blue, the clouds were white. Snow fell gently from time to time. There was scarcely a breath of wind.

Pooper flourished. On Saturdays and Sundays Andrew managed to spend hours playing with him in the snowy fields beyond the stream. If the tobogganing children asked, "Where's Andrew gone to?" John would say, "Oh, he'll be back" or "He wanted to take care of something." From time to time Andrew would appear on the slope and do some tobogganing, then he'd fade away when no one was looking. Sometimes John came to play with Pooper, too. But Andrew liked it better when he and Pooper were alone.

Of course, Andrew stopped going to the Saturday film show, although John and Jenny and Anne still went. He explained to his parents that he preferred to toboggan.

"That's the stuff," said his father. "You make the most of it. The snow won't last forever."

When his father said this, Andrew's stomach heaved. When the snow melted, what excuse could he give for going to the field so often? Birds' eggs. He'd say he was starting an egg collection. Or butterflies. Or wild flowers. Grown-ups always seemed pleased if children were keen on nature. But what was going to happen when his money for dog food ran out? Well, something would turn up.

Andrew gave Mrs. Walters all the money from his piggy bank, to buy dog food with. Of course, Andrew's mother finally discovered that the piggy bank was empty.

"It's for a surprise," mumbled Andrew, blushing beetroot red.

"What sort of surprise? You know you're not to spend that money without asking."

"Wait and see," said Andrew, trying to look mysterious. He succeeded, too, because his mother smiled and said, "Is it a birthday?" And

Andrew nodded and put on the sort of face that he imagined boys put on when they buy their mothers expensive birthday presents. He never bought his mother expensive presents. Somehow he never wanted to. It had something to do with how she nagged him and wished he were a girl. Anyway, her birthday wasn't for weeks.

Mrs. Walters was wonderful. Every afternoon after school Andrew knocked on her back door. She always smiled at him and asked him into her warm, untidy kitchen. She made him a quick cup of cocoa and he said hello to the baby. He asked if Mr. Elliot had been snooping and Mrs. Walters always replied that there had been no sign of him. Andrew told Mrs. Walters how Pooper could balance sugar on his nose; how Pooper "begged" for his dinner; how Pooper had stopped messing up the car and waited until Andrew came to let him out in the early morning. But Andrew could never explain properly how he loved Pooper or how Pooper loved him.

Sometimes Mr. Walters would be there. He would puff his pipe and listen and smile and say, "Don't fret about old man Elliot. If he goes sticking his big nose in, I'll punch it for him." Andrew loved feeling, for once, that some grown-ups were on his side.

The days went by in a sort of dream. The weather stayed glorious, with sun, snow, and blue skies. No one came from the houses. No child strayed through the wood. Anne and Jenny suspected nothing. John was a real friend, covering Andrew's tracks. Now that Andrew was going out of his way to please her, his mother nagged less and stopped complaining that Andrew was getting up too early. Andrew's father was pleased because Andrew and his mother were getting on so much better.

One week. Two weeks. Andrew was full of lovely plans. When the snow was gone and the Easter vacation had come, he would take Pooper for long rambles over the fields, away from the houses and sidewalks and horrible men with umbrellas. Pooper could tunnel through the long grass and bob up every now and then to make sure Andrew was following. Of course Andrew would be following. He would always follow Pooper.

Saturday, March 1, Andrew slept until seven. He woke feeling marvelously happy. There was a whole wonderful day ahead of him. His mother wouldn't expect him home until lunchtime. He had five marvelous hours to play with Pooper. And another five glorious hours after lunch. Andrew took a deep breath. How wonderful everything was.

He put on his Pooper clothes. In the kitchen he ate two pieces of bread and marmalade. He picked up his tray and went out. A thaw was beginning, there was no doubt about it. Water flowed from the dwindling piles of snow in the gutters. A blanket of snow fell off a roof with a *woomph*. When Andrew reached the building site, he saw that the planks and bricks and machines were losing their snowy covers. The potholes were full not of snow but of water. Mud squelched under his boots.

Andrew climbed the slope, which was showing green in the toboggan tracks. He wriggled through the hedge. He waded through the soft snow in the wood. He came out of the trees. He gave his special whistle. He stared. He whistled again.

No white shape bobbed up behind the window of the car.

9

There was no Pooper jumping up at the window.

Andrew whistled again. No Pooper. He dropped his tray. He hurled himself down to the stream. The stream was swollen and rapid. The stepping-stones were awash. Andrew jumped on a stone. He slipped, and one leg plunged thigh-deep into the water. The water plucked at his leg. His submerged boot felt like a ton weight. He got a grip on another stone. He pulled. The stone shifted, toppled, and tipped over with a huge splash. Andrew clung to the stone that his other leg rested on. By inches he dragged himself up. Trembling, he stepped on the last two stones and reached the bank. He ran lopsided to the car, calling, "Pooper!" He seized the handle and opened the door. He ducked and climbed in.

Pooper wasn't there.

Pooper was gone.

The straw stirred. Andrew crawled to the straw. His heart leaped with joy. Pooper was there! He was stretched out in the straw, asleep.

"Pooper," said Andrew. "Time to get up, you

lazybones. Come on, boy."

Pooper did not move.

Pooper was dead.

Andrew put a trembling hand on Pooper's side. No, he wasn't dead. He was breathing. He was warm. Overjoyed, Andrew pushed his hands under Pooper's body and tried to rouse him. How hot Pooper was. How fast his heart was thumping.

"Pooper! Pooper, it's me."

Pooper sighed. An eyelid trembled and slowly lifted. Andrew lay down and stared into Pooper's eye. It was dull, like a dark stone. There was no spark in it. Andrew slid his hand under Pooper's head and lifted it off the straw. He looked at the other eye. It was open, dull, without a spark.

Andrew felt terribly afraid. Pooper was ill. Pooper was very ill. "Pooper!" he cried again. Pooper's tail stirred. His head shifted a fraction in Andrew's hand. Pooper sighed again. His eyes closed. Andrew laid Pooper's head in the straw. He smoothed Pooper's eyebrows. He rubbed the backs of Pooper's ears. There was no response. Pooper lay like a dead dog, his mouth open a crack and spit running out of it.

Andrew ran like a mad thing down to the

Walterses' house. He banged on the back door and cried for Mrs. Walters. No one came. He ran around and beat on the front door and shouted, "Mrs. Walters! Mrs. Walters!"

No one came.

Andrew tried the back again. He noticed a bit of paper showing under the back door. He pulled it out. He read, "My mother's been taken ill again. We've gone to see her. Will be back Sunday. Food under back window. M. Walters."

Andrew began to cry. He leaned his forehead against the door. Who could help him? Who could help Pooper? He let the paper drop. He wandered around to the front of the house. A rough voice shouted, "What d'you think you're up to? What's all the flaming row?"

A huge shape loomed up. It was dressed in a brown robe and a gray overcoat and boots and a blue-and-red-striped scarf.

It was Mr. Tattooed Elliot.

Andrew stammered, "I only wanted Mr. and Mrs. W-w-w-walters."

Mr. Elliot shouted, "D'you know what the time is? Half past seven. What you making that horrible racket at half past seven for?"

Andrew said, "I'm going, I'm going." He sidled past Mr. Elliot and walked away from the field, away from Pooper.

Mr. Elliot shouted after him, "I know you.

Causing a disturbance, that's what you're doing. Oh, I know you. You just watch your step. I'll put the police on you."

Andrew ran. When Mr. Elliot was out of sight, he stopped and leaned against a lamppost. What could he do? Whom could he ask for help? John wouldn't know what to do. His parents would insist on telling the police and the police would take Pooper away and Andrew's heart would be broken. Andrew stood upright. No. He would tell nobody. Except John, of course. Today he would look after Pooper himself. Tomorrow Mr. and Mrs. Walters would come back and make Pooper better.

Andrew pulled off his boot and emptied the water out of it. He stamped his foot back into his boot. He squared his shoulders and dried his eyes on his gloves. He walked back toward the field. Hidden in the snow under the Walterses' back window he found crackers, crusts, a can of dog food and half a pint of milk. Carrying these, he made his way back to Pooper.

"It's all right, boy. I'll look after you. You'll soon be better. Mr. Walters will be home tomorrow. He'll know what to do. Here, drink this lovely milk, Pooper."

But Pooper couldn't even lift his head. Andrew lifted it for him and dribbled milk into Pooper's mouth. But Pooper couldn't swallow it, and it

trickled away through the straw. Andrew pushed a morsel of cracker into Pooper's mouth. Pooper let it lie there. Andrew opened the can and offered Pooper a scrap of meat on the end of his finger. Pooper didn't even twitch his nose. He lay motionless in the straw, burning hot. His breath panted. His heart thumped inside his ribs.

All morning Andrew sat beside Pooper in the car, watching and listening. He was dreadfully afraid. The sun melted more patches of snow off the windows. The clock ticked. Pooper panted.

Sometimes he sighed. Once he opened his eyes. Perhaps he was dying. Suppose he died before Mr. and Mrs. Walters came back?

All of a sudden Andrew could bear it no longer. He couldn't sit doing nothing, watching Pooper suffer. He must get some medicine to make Pooper better. John could not go. John was at the Saturday morning movies. Andrew must go himself.

He packed straw around Pooper, offered him milk, kissed him, and went out. It was eleven o'clock. As he approached the swollen stream he heard an engine turning over. It was a car over by the houses. Andrew stumbled to the lane and ran as fast as he could toward them. He saw a green car turning in a gateway. Its back tires were spraying slush and mud. He banged on the window.

A young man lowered the window. "What's up, son?"

"Can you give me a lift?"

"Where to?"

"To town."

"What's the matter? You've been crying. Someone hurt you?"

"No. I'm just late."

"Hop in, then."

Andrew ran around and got in. The young man started the engine. He let out the brake and spun the wheel and drove off. He bumped the car down a long lane and out onto a road. He stepped on the gas. The tires went swish-swish on the wet road. Andrew sat silent, thinking of Pooper, hot and panting in the straw.

"This do?" asked the young man when they reached the center of the town.

Andrew got out. He said, "Do you know where there's a vet?"

"Why? You got an animal ill?"

"No," said Andrew in a panic. "It's for my sister. I've got to get some pills for her cat."

"Well, there's Dr. Hopkins by the post office. That's near—"

But Andrew had gone.

He darted across the road, nearly under the wheels of a yellow truck. He ran along the wet pavement, sweating in his two sweaters and his wet jeans and his sopping boot. Outside the post office he looked frantically around. There it was. The window was covered with white Venetian blinds. On the glass door, gold lettering said: "Hopkins & Shortwood, Veterinary Surgeons." Andrew pushed open the door and went in. The door closed with a sigh behind him. The room was green, with green-and-black linoleum on the floor and benches around the walls. On one bench sat an old woman in a pink head scarf. She was holding a cardboard box on her knee. The box

was jumping around. Andrew tapped on a little window that said: "Information." The glass slid back.

"Yes?" said a girl in a blue uniform.

"Can I see the vet?"

"Have you brought an animal?"

"No. But it's about my dog. He's ill and I want—"

"We can't prescribe unless we see the animal, sonny."

"But he's ill!" cried Andrew. "I couldn't bring

him, he's too ill."

The girl said, "If you leave your name and address, Dr. Hopkins or Dr. Shortwood will come and see your dog."

"But he can't. I only want some pills. Please—"

A side door opened and a man in a white coat came out. Andrew went up to him and said, "My dog's ill. Please give me some pills for him."

The girl stuck her head through the window and said, "This lady is next, Dr. Hopkins."

The old woman said, "That's all right, dear. I don't mind waiting. The little boy's all upset."

Dr. Hopkins asked, "What's the matter, son?"

"My dog's very ill. He's hot and he won't drink, and I want some pills to make him better."

Dr. Hopkins was very kind, very understanding. He made Andrew sit down on a bench and he explained very patiently that he could not prescribe medicine for an animal he had not seen. "Tell me where you live and I will come and see your dog this afternoon," he said.

But of course Andrew could not tell him. If he told him, Dr. Hopkins would come to Andrew's house and it would all come out about Pooper living in the car and then Andrew's mother . . .

Andrew was too miserable to speak. He shook his head, sniffed, gulped, sobbed, and ran out of the office.

10

Andrew forced himself to go home for his lunch. His father had already gone off to see a friend. Andrew's mother was busy tying Anne's ribbons and polishing Anne's shoes, because she was taking Anne to see their aunt. "Your lunch is in the oven, Andrew," she called as she bustled Anne into her best coat in the hall. "Leave the key under the mat. And don't stay out late, we'll be back about six." They went out and banged the front door.

Andrew's mother very seldom took Andrew to his aunt's. But she took Anne quite often. She thought he was too sloppy, he supposed. Not that he wanted to go. But sometimes he thought it would be nice to be asked.

But not now, of course. Now every minute, every second belonged to Pooper. Andrew took off his wet boots and put on dry socks and his mother's brown boots. From the refrigerator he took a slice of brown bread and a slice of white bread, an apple and an orange (he hoped his mother hadn't kept count of them), and a slice of cheese. He took his lunch out of the oven and turned off the gas. It was a casserole. He tipped it into a plastic bag. He put all the food in a large paperbag and sandwiched it between his sweaters. He wrote, "Do not worry. I am O.K." on his mother's shopping list. He put a box of matches and three candles in his coat pocket. He put on his gloves and his hood and he let himself out the back door. He locked the door and slid the key under the mat.

John was waiting for him with his tin tray under his arm. "Where's your tray?" he asked. "Aren't you going to toboggan at all?"

"Pooper's ill," said Andrew, trying not to cry again.

John looked shocked and anxious. "Really ill, you mean?"

Andrew nodded. He said, "I'm going to stay the night with him."

"What, in the car?"

"Yes."

"You can't."

"Why not?"

"They won't let you."

"They won't know. You won't tell, will you?"

"Course I won't. But they'll worry."

"I've got to stay with Pooper. He needs me. Dogs need people when they're ill."

"When are you going?"

"Now."

"Make sure someone doesn't spot you."

"I'm going another way."

"Can I come?"

"Better not. We can't both be missing."

Andrew made a long detour to avoid both the Elliots and the tobogganers. He went down strange streets and along a path with high fences. He went under a low tunnel and came out on a ridge. He turned left and plodded through wet snow that clung to his mother's boots. He longed to hurry, but he was tired and wretched and sweating. The casserole squelched against his chest. His stomach rumbled. The sun was scorching. All around him water drip-dripped and snow ran away in little rivers.

He reached the wood and slid down to the stream. It was twice as wide as usual. He was astonished at the force of the water. It rocketed past, looking deep and black. As he stood there, the water rose four or five inches to touch his boot toes. He looked at the car. The snow had nearly all melted away from it. He walked along the bank to the crossing place. The crossing stones had vanished. How was he to get over?

Andrew scrambled up into the wood. Frantically he searched for a branch wide enough and long enough to act as a bridge. At last he found one. It was covered with mold, but it seemed strong. He dragged it to the edge of the wood and sent it crashing down the slope to the stream. He followed it. With an enormous effort he stood the branch on end. It poised for a second, then fell across the water.

Andrew took off his boots and threw them over the stream; they barely made it to the opposite bank. He stuffed his socks in his pockets. He stepped onto the branch. It rocked but it did not roll. It lay a few inches clear of the racing water. With thumping heart Andrew walked along the branch, like a tightrope walker crossing Niagara Falls. Once he staggered and nearly fell, but the branch shifted and he regained his balance. He dug his toes into the rough bark. He placed one bare foot in front of the other. Then he made a wild leap and landed on the bank. He rushed barefoot to the car. He crawled in. There was Pooper, just as he had left him. The stalk of straw that had been sticking up behind Pooper's left ear was still sticking up. Pooper hadn't stirred. He lay there with his eyes closed and his legs limp. His mouth was ajar, and spit dribbled out of it.

Andrew laid his ear on Pooper's side. There was breath in there but it was scarcely swelling Pooper's chest. Andrew felt Pooper's nose. It was hot and dry. He felt Pooper's heartbeats. They were faint, as if Pooper's heart were knocking a long way away.

Andrew put on his socks and his mother's boots. He extracted the pulpy paper bag from his sweaters. He offered Pooper water, milk, dog food, crackers, casserole, bread. It was no good, Pooper did not even open an eye. When Andrew trickled water down his throat, Pooper could not swallow it.

Andrew wound the clock. It was three fifteen. He put the candles and the matches in the glove compartment. Then he lay down with his head on the straw beside Pooper and his feet under the steering wheel. He heard the clock ticking. He heard the breath struggling inside Pooper's lungs. He heard water rushing past with the force of a cataract. He heard snow drip-drip-dripping. He closed his eyes. He smelled Pooper's doggy smell. He felt Pooper's heat burning his cheek. He sighed, opened his eyes, closed them, fell asleep.

When he awoke it was quite dark. He was stone cold. He pressed close to Pooper. Pooper's breath was still faintly struggling. Pooper's heart was still faintly beating. Andrew crawled to the glove compartment. He felt for, and lit, a candle. He held the candle above Pooper. "Don't die, Pooper," he begged. "Pooper, don't die." He lifted one of Pooper's eyelids. Underneath, the eyeball was rolled up nearly out of sight. Andrew looked at the clock. Eight o'clock. They would have missed him by now. They would be asking the neighbors, questioning John, questioning Peter Johnson. They would be out looking for him in scarves and gloves and boots. He was safe here. No one would find him here. No one must find him. If they found him they would take Pooper away and Andrew would never see him again. Pooper was safe here with Andrew to look after him. Pooper would recover. He would be better in the morning. He *would* get better.

For hours Andrew crouched beside his sick dog. The candle burned out and Andrew lit another. Outside, the stream roared. Inside, Pooper

battled for breath. Bubbles formed around his mouth. Every few minutes something clicked in his throat. Andrew pictured his father smoking endless cigarettes and biting his nails. He pictured his mother all red and cross. He pictured John standing in his blue pajamas and saying, "No, I don't know where he is," over and over again. He pictured a policeman. A policeman? Yes, they would call in the police. Parents always called the police when their children were missing. The police would send cars out. But no police car could reach here. No policeman would find this place. Pooper would be safe. He would get better.

But Pooper did not get better. As the hours passed, his breathing became more frantic. It was as if there were only a pinhole for his breath to go in and out of.

Andrew began to cry. He longed to breathe for Pooper. Between sobs he breathed in-out, in-out. He opened Pooper's mouth and blew down his windpipe, but his own breath came back in his face.

Ten o'clock. Eleven o'clock. Midnight. Something rattled in Pooper's throat. All at once Andrew knew what he had to do. He must save Pooper. He must carry Pooper home. If Pooper stayed here, he would die. Without medicine he would die.

But if Andrew carried Pooper home, he would

have to give Pooper up. Pooper could not live in the housing project. He would be taken away and Andrew would never see him again.

Nevertheless, Andrew must carry Pooper home so that the vet could come and give him medicine and make him better. Pooper must not die. That was the most important thing.

Andrew pulled off his boots and his socks. He opened the door and pushed it back against the body of the car. He crawled back to the corner. He unfastened his coat. He tucked his sweaters into his jeans. He buckled his belt as tight as he could. He pulled down the V's of his sweaters and with his right hand he took hold of Pooper's back legs. He lay down level with the straw and maneuvered Pooper inch by inch inside his sweaters. He arranged Pooper's head so that Pooper could breathe—but how feeble that breath was!

Andrew fastened his coat. He put on his gloves and his hood. He picked up his boots and his socks. He blew out the candle. He crawled to the door. Burdened with Pooper, he stepped out.

He plunged knee-deep into swirling water.

11

The stream had flooded. The car was surrounded by water.

Andrew staggered. He pressed his back against the car. He felt the car rock. Soon it would be afloat. He was terrified. He knew he must step out into the water that he could feel plucking his feet and his knees. There was only one way he could go. That was away from the bed of the stream and toward the houses. He would have to wake that young man. The young man would take him and Pooper home in the car.

He edged to his left. Pooper sagged against him. "It's all right, boy. I'll look after you, Pooper." Andrew slid his back along the body of the car. His left hand fastened on the knob of the radiator. His thighs felt the jagged rim of the mudguard. He edged around the radiator, while the water pulled greedily at his legs. Clinging with both hands, he reached the far side of the car. He could see nothing, not even the water that was trying to carry him and Pooper away. "Don't worry, Pooper. I'll soon have you safe." Under his chin, Pooper's head did not stir.

Andrew braced his back against the car. He knew he must be facing the lane and the houses. He took a deep breath and stepped out. The force of the water staggered him. The water was above his knees. Walking was like wading in a strong sea. He swayed. He gripped with his toes and recovered his balance. He began to battle in what he hoped was the right direction. He was blindfolded by the night. He was deafened by the roar of the flood. With each step he took he could feel his foot being carried away from the straight line. Soon he did not know which way he was facing. The water was up to his groin. It jumped against his stomach as if it wanted to snatch Pooper away from him. He could scarcely keep upright. He had lost all sense of direction. In his terror he cried out.

Above the roar of the water he heard a shout. Ahead, he saw flashes of light. Flashlights! Men! He tried to hurry toward them. He lost his footing and fell. The water rolled over him. He rose, gasping. He plunged his hand into his coat and raised Pooper's sopping head. More shouts. Eyes of yellow light. He fought the current. The eyes swung to and fro in an arc. Words faintly reached him. "Go back! Go back!" Go back? But he must reach the lights. "Go back!" Then the truth hit him. The men and the lights were on the other side of the stream. He was going the wrong way. In struggling toward them he was struggling toward the depths of the flood. He staggered around and battled in the opposite direction. He was exhausted. He could scarcely move his legs. He wanted to lie down and float away on the black water with Pooper.

He struggled on.

The ground dropped away. He plunged into a pit of water. Icy water closed over his head. He kicked out and shot to the surface, gasping for air. He whirled around and around. He flung out his arms. His hands hit something, clutched something. He drew up his legs. His bare feet found a hold. Painfully he pulled himself up, so that Pooper might not drown. Knives cut into his feet, but his hands were safe inside their leather gloves and he hauled himself and Pooper up and up, out of the sucking water.

He was in a hedge. He clung there while the flood raged around him. With one hand he managed to raise Pooper's wet head. He lowered his cheek to Pooper's mouth. Pooper was breathing! That was all that mattered. Soon the men with flashlights would come and everything would be over.

They came. They came rowing down the lane in a boat and they found Andrew draped in the hedge like wet laundry. They lifted him into the

boat and exclaimed in astonishment when they found a little dog inside his clothes. They tried to take Pooper away but Andrew clung to Pooper and would not let them take him.

Andrew lay in the rocking boat. It was like a nightmare, the blackness and the ridges of the boat and the yellow eyes of the flashlights. He heard voices shouting, "This way," and "There's the house," and "How's the boy?" and "He'll do, but the dog's a goner."

The boat grounded. Andrew was lifted out and

carried to a car. "Bring him in the house, he's half-drowned." "No, better get him home."

Andrew shut his eyes as two blinding suns sprang out of the darkness. Men hoisted him. Pooper's sopping head fell against his neck. He was handed feet first into the car. A door slammed. The car rocked. Another door slammed. The engine burst into life and the car drove off. Andrew lay sprawled across men's knees with Pooper on his chest. He tried to shift Pooper. A man said, "Take it easy, son. We'll soon have you home." Lights flashed across his face. Water trickled down his neck. He felt cold and clammy. His feet hurt. Pooper lay like a dead weight on his chest.

The car stopped. The door opened. There was a chorus of voices. Someone was crying. Hands patted his legs. He heard a child say, "I didn't tell, Andrew. Mr. Elliot told them. I didn't tell where you were." He was lifted out and carried into his own house and laid on the sofa; and Pooper still lay on him like a dead thing. Andrew was worried about his mother's sofa being spoiled. He saw his mother. She was crying! But his mother never cried. He said, "Please help Pooper. Please make Pooper better. Please . . ."

Then the room vanished and Andrew was whisked away in a black whirlwind.

When he awoke he stared at a ceiling bright

with sunlight. His own ceiling. He tried to move his hands to his chest, to feel if Pooper was there. To his surprise his hands would not move. He tried to lift his head to see if Pooper still lay on him. But his head wouldn't lift. He took a deep breath. His chest swelled. That meant Pooper wasn't there. Where was Pooper? Was he better? Had they taken him away? Was he dead? Andrew tried to sit up. Nothing happened. He tried to shout. A croak came out of his mouth.

His mother's face appeared above him. It was red and puffy. She said, "You've been asleep for a very long time."

"Where's Pooper?"

She bent and fiddled with the blanket.

"Mom, where's my dog?"

She said, "You've been asleep for thirteen hours, did you know? The doctor's coming again this afternoon."

"Mom, where's Pooper? What's happened to Pooper?"

She moved out of sight. Andrew heard clinkings. She returned with a glass of water and two white pills. "Now you just shallow these. The doctor said." She raised his head, but he wouldn't open his mouth. Through clenched teeth he muttered, "Where's Pooper? Where's my dog?"

His mother sighed. She laid him down. She said, "I'm afraid the dog's very ill." Andrew stared at her. She said, "The vet has him. The policeman took the dog to the vet's house last night. He was very nice, that policeman. He came before lunch to ask how you were. He says the dog's very ill but the vet's doing what he can."

Andrew shut his eyes. A tear trickled down over his ear. His mother's hand stroked his forehead. It felt quite soft and gentle. "Take your pills," she said. She propped up his head and he swallowed the pills.

All afternoon Andrew lay in bed, worrying and worrying. His arms and legs came back to life. He tossed around in his hot bed, frantic with worry about Pooper. "Pooper," he muttered over and over again. His father came and peeped at him and patted his shoulder, holding his cigarette behind his back. Anne tiptoed in and was shooed out again. His mother crept around with damp washcloths and pills and glasses of water.

The doctor came. He listened to Andrew's chest and counted his pulse and took his temperature. "Pooper," moaned Andrew. He felt the jab of a needle, and he dropped into sleep.

For two days and two nights Andrew tossed and croaked. He suffered dreadful nightmares in which Pooper was in terrible danger and Andrew was unable to reach him.

Then at last Andrew woke up. There was a heavy weight on his chest. He lifted his head— and there was Pooper! There was his very own Pooper, lying on Andrew's chest with his paws on Andrew's shoulders. "Oh, Pooper!" Andrew put his arms around Pooper and hugged him and hugged him. And Pooper wriggled close and licked Andrew's face and whined with joy. An-

drew kissed Pooper and sat him up. Yes, it was
his own darling dog, with bright black eyes and a
white-and-brown coat and tufty eyebrows and a
ruff and twenty-nine whiskers, fourteen on one
side and fifteen on the other.

Andrew refused to think of the future. Pooper
was safe, when he could have been drowned.
Pooper was cured, when he could have been dead.
He said, "Oh Pooper, I'm so glad." Later, Pooper
fell fast asleep on the quilt; and Andrew's mother
did not say a word.

12

Andrew's father tapped his ash into the hearth. He said, "You know the rule, son. No dogs in the development. Pooper's only been allowed to stay this long because the doctor wrote a special letter. Now that you're better, the dog'll have to go." He looked at Andrew curled up in the corner of the sofa with Pooper in his lap.

Andrew's mouth trembled. He said bravely, "Couldn't we live somewhere else, Dad?"

Two lines creased his Dad's forehead. He tapped his cigarette again, although the ash was not ready to drop. He got half up, then sat down again. He drew deeply on his cigarette and blew out the smoke in two jets from his nose. He said, "Andrew, you are ten years old. You can understand things. Do you know how long your mother and I waited to get this project house? Eight years. Eight years! I put our name on the waiting list the week Anne was born. Eight years we lived in that crummy apartment, waiting for a house."

"It wasn't crummy," said Andrew.

His father looked at him and plucked his lower lip with a cigarette-stained finger.

Andrew said, "Well, it wasn't too bad." But he remembered the cracked bathtub and the landlady who banged on the ceiling and the twenty-three slippery iron steps down to the yard.

Andrew's father leaned forward in his chair. He said, "I can't ask your mother to go back to that, Andrew. She loves having a nice house and two bathrooms and a decent kitchen and everything. Anyway, an apartment isn't suitable for a dog. Most apartments won't have dogs."

"Couldn't you buy a house, Dad?"

His father sighed. He threw his cigarette in the fire. "A house not half as nice as this costs much more than we can afford. I haven't even got enough for a deposit. Use your head, son."

Andrew rested his head on the back of the sofa. He said in a trembly voice, "What'll happen to Pooper, then?"

"Oh, we'll find a good home for him, never fear. We'll put an advertisement in the paper. We'll find kind people to take him. He's a nice little dog, I must say."

"When?" asked Andrew faintly.

"When what?"

"When's he got to go?"

"End of the week. The housing manager said. Pooper must be out of here by Saturday. You're lucky to be able to keep him that long. It's been more than a week."

Andrew lay down with his face against the back of the sofa. Pooper wriggled onto Andrew's hip. Pooper's leg slipped and Andrew tucked it up in case his mother should get cross about white hairs on the furniture. Not that his mother showed any signs of getting cross. It was amazing. She hadn't once scolded Andrew for sleeping in the car or for secreting Pooper there. She hadn't nagged about muddy paws or the chewed corner of Andrew's quilt. She hadn't mentioned Andrew's soaked clothes or her lost tin tray. She had even bought a collar and a lead and she had allowed Anne to take Pooper for little walks, not that he had wanted to go, not without Andrew.

Andrew's father noticed that Andrew shifted Pooper's leg. He said, "You know, son, your mother was real upset when you were missing."

"I left a note."

"Frantic, your mother was."

"Not as bad as if it was Anne."

"Now there you're wrong, Andrew. I've thought she favored Anne a bit, I'll confess. But not anymore."

Andrew turned his head.

His father went on, "D'you know what your mother said when we couldn't find you? She said, 'What'll I do without him?' "

"She didn't!"

"She did. She was crying and she kept saying, 'What'll I do without him?' Honest, son. Your mother thinks a lot of you, though she's not always shown it, I'll agree."

Andrew said slowly, "Do you reckon she'd let me keep Pooper? I mean, if I *could* keep him?"

"Not a doubt of it. Quite won her heart Pooper has. She gave him a kiss yesterday."

"She didn't!"

"She did. Could have knocked me down with a feather." With the tongs, Andrew's father stirred the fire and then lit another cigarette.

Andrew closed his eyes. He was glad about his mother. He would have been so happy if only . . .

The days went by quickly. Too quickly. Andrew began staying up for dinner. Andrew began taking Pooper out for walks with John. They went to see the flood. It was still wide and deep. The old car had been washed away.

John said, "I didn't tell. The policeman asked at all the houses and the Walterses were away and Mr. Elliot said he'd seen you acting suspicious in the field, so the policeman got men to go searching and they found the gap in the hedge and the stream and the car and then they rescued you."

Mr. and Mrs. Walters and the baby came to see Andrew, to hear all about his adventure and to return to him what was left of his dog-food money. Andrew's mother was very nice to them. She didn't blame them for not telling anybody that Andrew was keeping a dog in the old car. She insisted on buying Mrs. Walters another clock and two more red plastic bowls. And she gave the baby a bag of chocolate candy and a new shovel.

Every day Andrew asked his father if he'd put the ad in the paper. You see, Andrew was hoping for another miracle, like the miracle when Pooper appeared in the snow. He simply could not believe that people were going to separate him from Pooper. People couldn't be so cruel. It would be like cutting one of Andrew's arms off.

One day his father said, "Yes, I've put it in."

"Have you had any answers?"

"Not yet."

Thursday. Friday. Andrew's last day with his dog.

On Friday evening, when Andrew's father came home, he said, "Pooper's lucky, son. There's a nice young fellow who wants to have him. I've got to take him after dinner. Do you want to come?"

Andrew snatched up Pooper and ran away to his room. He lay on his bed, crying. Pooper burrowed under his master's arm as if he wanted to hide. Andrew heard his mother giving his father his dinner. Soon his father came in with Pooper's lead. "Come on, son. You want to see where Pooper's going, don't you?"

Andrew got up and blew his nose and put on his coat. He fastened Pooper's lead. Pooper didn't frisk or bark. He knew. Andrew and Pooper and his father went downstairs. Andrew's mother came out of the living room. She kissed Andrew on the cheek. She looked pink, as if she expected something to happen. Inside the room Anne squealed and Andrew's mother hurried back in and shut the door.

Outside, the snow was all gone. The air was mild. The world smelled of spring. The grass was a vivid green. The front doors gleamed red and blue and yellow and green. Housewives stood on chairs polishing the outsides of their windows. Husbands polished their already shining cars. On the clean sidewalks there was not a single candy paper or cigarette package. When Andrew's father lit another cigarette, he put the used match in his pocket.

They went to the bus stop. Andrew saw John. John looked as if he were going to speak, then he suddenly walked away. Andrew and his father and Pooper got on the bus. Andrew thought, "It can't be happening. They can't really be taking Pooper away from me."

They rode to the center of the town. Pooper lay down under the seat and rested his chin on

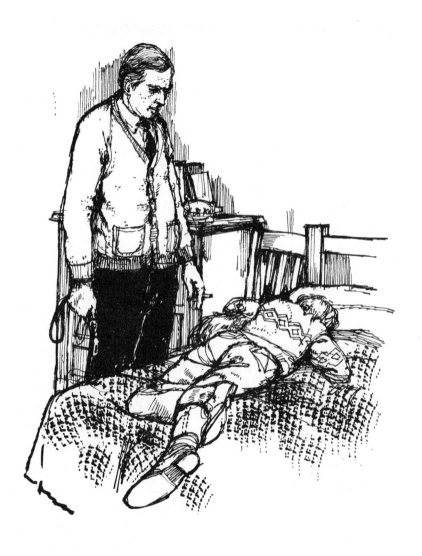

Andrew's shoes. He was trembling. He knew what was happening. Andrew stared out of the window. He tried not to cry.

At the bus station they changed buses. They sat down again and Pooper lay down, trembling, under the seat. His trembles made Andrew tremble. Andrew stared out of the window. Now they were riding along grubby streets. Here, all the houses were joined in sixes. They looked poky and shabby. They were built of purple bricks. Their front doors were blistered. Their windows were minute. Their tiny front gardens were enclosed by straggly privet hedges. There were very few cars in these streets.

"Wouldn't think this was a project, would you?" said Andrew's Dad. "But it is. Built before the war. Nothing like ours, eh?"

They got off the bus. Andrew's father led the way down a side street. Pooper trailed behind, his collar up around his ears. A black dog bounded across the street ahead of them. Pooper paid no attention. He did not even sniff the lampposts. Andrew kept his eyes on the pavement. It was littered with cigarette packages and dirty papers.

"Here we are," said Andrew's father, stopping by a parked motorcycle. He pushed open a rickety gate. He walked up the path. Andrew forced himself to follow, pulling Pooper behind him. It couldn't be happening; they couldn't be taking Pooper away from him.

Andrew's father pushed the bell. The door opened. A man with a bald pink head stood in the doorway. He smiled. He said, "Come in, Mr. Thornton."

Andrew's father stepped inside. Andrew's feet would not carry him over the threshold. The bald man came out and led him and Pooper into the house. He shut the front door behind them. Andrew stood staring miserably at the floor. The man put his hand in the middle of Andrew's back. "In here," he said. Andrew picked Pooper up and carried him into the living room. Tears were running down his face. He hid his trembling chin in Pooper's coat.

There were a lot of people in the room. Andrew looked down at the carpet. There was a baby sitting on the carpet. It was Mrs. Walter's baby.

Andrew's heart jumped. Something was going to happen. He put Pooper down. He took off Pooper's lead and Pooper went and sniffed the baby's ear. What was happening? Andrew looked up. He saw Mrs. Walters. He saw Mr. Walters. He saw a young man with red hair. He saw a woman with gray hair sitting in an armchair with her feet on a stool. He looked from one person to another. He felt puzzled, excited. He didn't understand what was happening.

The bald man came in. He stood beside Andrew's father. He looked at Andrew's flushed face. He smiled and said, "Tell him, Margaret."

Mrs. Walters came up to Andrew. She picked Pooper up and put him in Andrew's arms. She said, "Andrew, these are my parents. This is where I used to live."

The gray-haired woman smiled and said, "How do you do, Andrew," and the bald man said, "Parkes is our name. Margaret was a Parkes, you see, until she married Jeff here." Mr. Walters waved from the fireplace.

Mrs. Walters said, "My mom and dad have made a switch."

Andrew didn't understand.

"My parents have swapped houses with your parents. My mom gets ill sometimes and we want her and my dad and Arnie to come live near us, so I can give her a hand when she's not well."

Andrew turned and looked at his father, who nodded and said, "That's right, son." Andrew looked at Mrs. Walters. He hitched Pooper onto his shoulder and Pooper licked his cheek and banged his tail against Andrew's hand.

Mrs. Walters picked up the baby, who was trying to climb up her legs. The baby lunged and clutched one of Pooper's ears. Mrs. Walters said, "You can keep a dog here, Andrew. This is an old project. They allow dogs here. Your parents have swapped houses with my parents so that you can keep Pooper." She paused. Nobody moved except the baby, who was making kissing noises into Pooper's ear.

Then Andrew's father blew out a jet of smoke and said, "Andrew, *you* are the nice young fellow I was telling you about, who wants to have Pooper. Well, what's the matter, son? Why don't you say something?"

Andrew was speechless. Pooper nosed Andrew's neck but for once Andrew ignored him. One thought obsessed him. It wasn't his sister Anne, who would miss Jenny so badly. It wasn't his friend John, who was old enough to come and play whenever he liked. It wasn't even Pooper. It was his mother he was thinking of.

His mother was giving up her beautiful shining new semidetached house. His mother was moving into a shabby old house. And she was doing it so that her sloppy son Andrew could keep his little dog.

"Well, aren't you glad, Andrew?"

A rocket exploded inside Andrew. He went wild. He dropped on his knees with Pooper and they tumbled and rolled together on the floor. Pooper broke free and yelped and danced, and everybody smiled and laughed and Andrew jumped up and shouted with joy. He held out his arms and cried, "Up, Pooper!" and Pooper leaped three feet into his master's grasp.

Mrs. Parkes opened the door. He said, "Have

a look around, son. There's a nice little garden
out in the back. It's all yours tomorrow."

Tomorrow? Andrew's dad said, "That's right.
We're moving in tomorrow."

Tomorrow. That meant Andrew need not be
parted from Pooper, not even for one day. The
miracle had happened. Pooper was Andrew
Thornton's dog forever and ever.

Andrew was too happy to speak. He walked
out into the hall, with Pooper trotting at his heels.
He went into the kitchen. He opened the back
door and Pooper bounded out and Andrew ran
after him into the garden.